DODO DODGEBALL

By Heidi E. Y. Stemple
Illustrated by Eva Byrne

Ready-to-Read

Simon Spotlight
New York London Toronto Sydney New Delhi

For Casey, Alex, and Jamie—dodos forever! —H. E. Y. S.
For Ronnie, with love xx —E. B.

SIMON SPOTLIGHT

An imprint of Simon & Schuster Children's Publishing Division

1230 Avenue of the Americas, New York, New York 10020

This Simon Spotlight edition May 2024

Text copyright © 2024 by Heidi E. Y. Stemple

Illustrations copyright © 2024 by Eva Byrne

SIMON SPOTLIGHT, READY-TO-READ, and colophon are registered trademarks of
Simon & Schuster, LLC.

Simon & Schuster: Celebrating 100 Years of Publishing in 2024

For information about special discounts for bulk purchases, please contact Simon & Schuster
Special Sales at 1-866-506-1949 or business@simonandschuster.com.

The Simon & Schuster Speakers Bureau can bring authors to your live event. For
more information or to book an event contact the Simon & Schuster Speakers Bureau
at 1-866-248-3049 or visit our website at www.simonspeakers.com.

Manufactured in the United States of America 0324 LAK

10 9 8 7 6 5 4 3 2 1

Library of Congress Cataloging-in-Publication Data

Names: Stemple, Heidi E. Y., author. | Byrne, Eva, illustrator. Title: Dodo dodgeball / by Heidi
E. Y. Stemple ; illustrated by Eva Byrne. Description: Simon Spotlight edition. | New York :
Simon Spotlight, 2024. | Series: Ready-to-read: Level 1 | Audience: Ages 4 to 6. | Audience:
Grades K-1. | Summary: While the ducks and dodos play dodgeball, Chick sits nearby
reading her book. Identifiers: LCCN 2023025386 (print) | LCCN 2023025387 (ebook) | ISBN
9781665952088 (paperback) | ISBN 9781665952095 (hardcover) | ISBN 9781665952101
(ebook) Subjects: CYAC: Stories in rhyme. | Ducks—Fiction. | Dodos—Fiction. | Pigeon family
(Birds)—Fiction. | Dodgeball—Fiction. | Ball games—Fiction. | Books and reading—Fiction.
| Humorous stories. | LCGFT: Stories in rhyme. | Animal fiction. | Humorous fiction. | Picture
books. Classification: LCC PZ8.3.S8228 Do 2024 (print) | LCC PZ8.3.S8228 (ebook) | DDC
[E]—dc23 LC record available at https://lccn.loc.gov/2023025386
LC ebook record available at https://lccn.loc.gov/2023025387

Tweet!

Ducklings and dodos
line up along the wall.

Coach Dodo picks two teams
for a game of dodo dodgeball.

Players face each other
in the center of the floor.

A new student enters

through the locker-room door.

"The rules are very simple. Throw the ball at the other team.

If you are hit,
then you are out.
We play for fun,
so do not be mean."

"Watch me, Coach Dodo!"

Chick sits in the corner
and opens up her book.

"Okay, players—
settle down.
We have a warm-up to do."

Chick turns a page, looks up and says,

I prefer to read.
No, thank you.

Ducklings stretch up high.

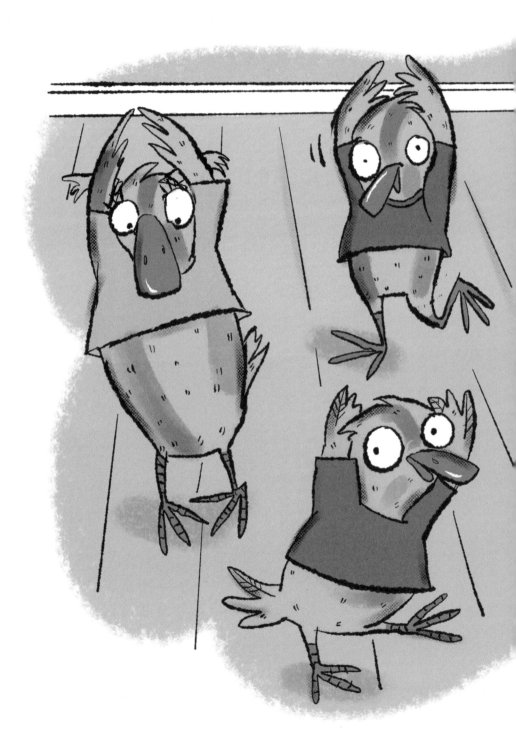

Dodos bend down low.

Warm-up is over,

Coach Dodo starts the game.

Tweet!

Both teams pick up
dodgeballs.
Ready, set,
take aim!

Dodos crash.

Thank you.

Ducklings bash.

All but one has been hit.

The dodgeball game is done.

The green team takes
a victory lap.

The dodgeball game is won!

But where are the bench
and trophy shelf?
Where is the chair?

"Dodos! Ducklings!"
Coach Dodo yells.
"Look over there!"

Dodos and ducklings
each grab a book.
Not one of them says no.

There is one book left,
a special one.
Chick hands it to Coach Dodo.